A GEEKS AND THINGS COZY MYSTERY

Debts and Debtors

S.E. BIGLOW

 Created with Vellum

1

Raindrops pelted the kitchen window in Kalina Greystone's small apartment. Heat from the kitchen fogged the interior of the glass, obscuring the view outside. Kalina wiped sweat from her forehead with the back of her arm. The weather—in addition to being wet—had turned cold in early November and she'd turned up the heat to compensate. She was up to her elbows in dessert. This was the first Thanksgiving she'd been home with her family in a few years—and the first since her father and Aunt Agatha's passing—and she didn't want to disappoint. Checking the recipe for the spice applesauce cake frosting one more time, she moved the saucepan of brown sugar, cream and butter to the burner set on high. It reached a boil in only a few minutes and she feverishly stirred it to make sure it didn't burn. Master cook she was not. Her phone buzzed with an incoming call, slowly vibrating toward the edge of the table.

"Not now!" she moaned, hastily pulling the concoction from the stove and scooping up her phone.

Luckily, it was just an alarm to remind her she needed to leave for Jillian's house in a half hour. Chris was supposed to be coming over so they could drive together. The thought of having her very serious romantic partner joining her for a family holiday made butter-flies swarm in her stomach. Things between them had been better than ever the last few months. In fact, they were in the process of moving in together. The process had been put on hold due to the holidays but before long she wouldn't have to live alone. Her front room was already strewn with partially packed boxes. Her landlord was being generous and letting her leave most of the furniture in the place. Easier to rent a fully furnished place in a town like this. She couldn't believe how lucky she'd been, moving home, taking over the family business and falling back in love with her high school sweetheart. Some days she had to pinch herself to make sure she wasn't dreaming.

Setting her phone aside, she added the remaining ingredients to the frosting mixture, gave it a good stir and carefully poured it over the cake. It still needed to cool a little bit but that's what her sister's fridge was for. Making sure the stovetop was off, she headed to her room to clean up. Ten minutes later she reappeared in a nice, pale blue blouse and black slacks. She slipped into rain boots and tossed a pair of flats into her purse.

She checked her phone, expecting a text from Chris letting her know he was waiting out front. No new messages. "Come on, where are you?"

Kalina busied herself packing up the cake and pulling on her jacket but still no word from Chris. Finally, she sent him a text. 'Are you on your way? We're going to be late.'

Still no response.

This was not the way she wanted to spend her Thanksgiving but she couldn't help feeling a little annoyed that he was suddenly ignoring her. Finally, she pulled on her coat and stowed her phone in her pocket for safe-keeping. Time to brave the storm.

Torrents of water buffeted her all the way to her car. She practically dove into the driver seat; the cake container almost landed side-ways on the passenger seat. She let out a breath—air condensing in front of her—and started the engine. She set the wipers on high and waited for the heat to kick in before she pulled out of the driveway and turned left down her street.

Her phone began to ring loudly halfway to Jillian's house. "Great."

Her mood already on edge, she pulled over to the side of the road and yanked the phone free. Chris's number flashed on the Caller ID. She hit 'Accept' and put the phone on speaker so she could keep driving. "Hey." She did her best to keep her tone neutral.

"I am so sorry, Kal."

"You can meet me there. That's fine."

"I don't think I can make it."

"You promised." It came out as more of a whine than she'd intended.

"I know. I wish I could be there, believe me. But I got called out to the beach for a case. I swear I will find a way to make it up to you."

She took several breaths before she responded. "Fine. I get it. You have to work. You can't choose when dead bodies turn up."

"Please don't be mad at me. I told the guys I was off today but Jimmy called last minute and said he needed my help on this one."

Kalina's anger softened a touch at the young officer's name. He was a good kid but eager to impress. She also wasn't above gently grilling him for information when she needed something. But that hadn't happened in months. She was trying to stay out of police matters. She was a comic book shop owner, after all. "Okay. I'll pass on your regrets to everyone."

"Thanks. I love you."

She smiled. "I love you too."

Easing to a stop at a crosswalk, she hit 'End' and set her phone aside. Her sister's house loomed up ahead on the side of town farthest from the beach. Jillian had insisted on staying local but when AJ had come along she'd wanted a yard too. Somehow, Kalina's older sister got exactly what she wanted. She was lucky that way. Even getting pregnant right out of college, Jillian managed to make it all work.

Through the downpour she spotted her mom's car in the driveway. She pulled up beside it and braced herself for the short trek to the front door. Pulling the hood of her coat up over her face, she grabbed the cake container and darted from the car. Thirty seconds later, she was safely inside the front hall being greeted by her nephew, AJ.

"It's really coming down out there," he said and took the container so she could peel her soaked jacket from her shoulders.

"It's insane. I wouldn't be surprised if it turned to snow later tonight." She leaned against the door to kick off her rain boots and put on her flats.

AJ lifted the lid of the container and took a sniff. "Where's Chris?"

"Working. He got called away on an urgent case."

"Lame."

"Behave yourself," she chided and quickly finger-combed her hair so she looked presentable before her sister appeared.

"AJ, put that in the kitchen," Jillian ordered. She stood a good four inches taller than Kalina and she'd inherited their mother's wavy curls and light brown hair.

No one would have ever accused them of being siblings, and yet they'd shared a bedroom until Jillian had gone off to college. They weren't especially close these days but Jillian seemed pleased that Kalina was keeping AJ out of trouble.

"Sorry I'm late ... and dateless," Kalina muttered.

"It's a hell of a storm out there. I'm just glad you made it over safely." Jillian's facial features softened and she pulled her sister into an impromptu hug.

"How many glasses of wine have you had?" Kalina whispered.

"Shut up." Jillian pulled away but smiled. "Do you want red or white?"

"Whatever's open," Kalina said with a dismissive wave.

"Red it is."

Kalina followed her sister into the kitchen. Her brother-in-law, Daniel, stood by the stove dutifully stirring their mother's homemade gravy. He was a decent guy. He'd stuck with Jillian and married her after he'd gotten her pregnant. They seemed to have a solid marriage now. She had to give them both credit for sticking it out and really building something in the years since AJ came along.

"Hey, where's Mom?" Kalina asked, accepting the glass of wine Jillian hastily shoved into her hand.

"Living room. She's ... not handling things well today."

Kalina excused herself with a nod towards

the living room and disappeared. Her mother sat on the couch, staring out at the storm. She settled in beside her and leaned over to give her a kiss on the cheek.

"Hi, Mom. How are you?"

"Fine, sweetheart." She didn't look away from the window.

"Mom, come on, it's me. I know you miss him and Aunt Agatha. We all do."

Her mother turned to face Kalina with tears already staining her cheeks. "I thought I would be okay, having you girls with me. I'm so sorry."

Kalina set her glass down on the table and wrapped her mother in a hug. "You don't have anything to be sorry about, Mom. You have a good cry."

They sat together for a few minutes in silence, the only sound the occasional murmurs from the kitchen and the hammering of the rain outside. Kalina briefly wondered where her nephew had disappeared to but her curiosity died when a loud knock echoed from the front of the house. She didn't move, unsure whether it was a knock on the front door or if it was just the weather raging. When the sound came again—this time a more distinct knocking—she extricated herself from her mother's embrace and went to answer the door. A woman—maybe in her early forties—stood on the front porch, purse clutched to her chest. Her hair was matted to her scalp from the rain.

"Can I help you?"

"I'm looking for Jillian."

Kalina turned toward the kitchen and called, "Jillian, there's someone here for you."

Her sister appeared in view and immediately raced forward. "Come in, come in."

Kalina stepped out of the way, letting Jillian dote on their surprise guest. She waited to be introduced but in all of her fussing Jillian seemed to have forgotten the rest of the family. Even AJ had appeared—from his room it turned out—to survey the commotion.

"You want to introduce us, Jill?" Kalina asked.

Jillian blushed. "Sorry. This is Savannah Hennessey. We went to college together."

Savannah stood shivering and dripping on the welcome mat. "It's actually Chase now. Thomas and I got married a couple years ago." The mention of her marriage brought tears to Savannah's eyes and her lower lip quivered. "I think something awful has happened to my husband."

2

———

Awkward silence filled the front hall as everyone present processed Savannah's declaration. Kalina bit the inside of her lip at the realization that she'd been secretly itching for a new mystery to solve. She caught AJ's eye and he looked as eager as she felt. They were, of course, premature in their excitement. There was every possibility that there was no mystery in need of a solution.

"Why don't we get you out of those wet

clothes and you can tell us what's going on?" she said, taking charge of the situation. She turned to Jillian. "I'm sure you've got something she can borrow."

"Of course. You're right."

Jillian helped Savannah out of her coat and they disappeared upstairs to the master bedroom in search of dry clothes. Kalina shut the door and looked pointedly at her nephew. "Don't get ahead of yourself."

He held up his hands in a defensive posture. "I didn't say anything."

Daniel poked his head out of the kitchen. "I take it we'll be setting another place for dinner?"

"No. Well, just use Chris's place setting. He can't make it."

Her brother-in-law nodded and ducked back into the kitchen to tend to the meal. Kalina ushered AJ into the living room where her mother still sat on the couch. She looked a little perkier at least. They waited in silence for Jillian and her friend to come back downstairs. After what seemed like an hour but was likely only fifteen minutes, they reappeared. Savannah had blow-dried her hair and wore a sweater and jeans. They fit remarkably well. She'd clearly dried her eyes, too. Jillian carried a box of tissues as a precaution.

"So, what makes you think something's happened to your husband?" Kalina asked.

"I haven't seen him since yesterday morning. He always comes home, even if he's late. I started to get worried when he didn't come home at all. If he's going to be late at the office he always calls me. He knows I worry."

"Did you go to the police?"

Savannah shook her head. "No. I thought I had to wait forty-eight hours before I could report him missing."

"Actually, you can report after twenty-four," AJ piped up.

Jillian gave him a cross look and he closed

his mouth. "Well, either way, you should report it as soon as you can."

Savannah tugged at the ends of her hair. "They aren't working today."

Kalina couldn't help but feel a little bitter. "They're always working."

Outside the wind picked up to a vicious howl and rain slammed against the siding and windows. Lightning split the sky in vibrant arcs and thunder boomed not long after. The storm was far from over.

"I think you may have to wait until tomorrow. It isn't safe to be out in this weather," Kalina said.

Savannah sniffled and wrapped her arms around her torso. "He could be out there all alone. Why didn't he come home last night?" Fresh tears trickled down her cheeks.

Jillian disappeared into the kitchen and returned with a glass of wine, which she shoved into her friend's quivering grasp. She took several large swallows before setting it on the coffee table in front of her.

Daniel stuck his head out from the kitchen doorway. "Dinner is ready."

Jillian cleared her throat and ushered their mother and Savannah into the dining room. She motioned for Kalina to follow her back into the kitchen. AJ busied himself helping direct people to their seats.

"I meant to tell you that AJ can't work this weekend," Jillian said and handed Kalina a serving dish of mashed potatoes.

"And why's that?"

"He just needs some time at home, that's all."

"Well, that's not how a job works, Jill. You know that. You were the one who wanted him to take on more responsibility, get some actual job experience for his college applications, and that's what he's doing. If he needs the time off for school work then fine. But that request comes from him, not you. Mommy can't call him out sick in the real world."

"Kalina, that's not fair."

Kalina took a deep breath to calm her nerves. They didn't need to fight, especially not in front of their mother. She was emotionally fragile as it was given the nature of the holiday. Kalina carried the dish to the table and set it between the green beans and stuffing. Making one last trip to the kitchen, she poured herself another glass of wine and settled in at the table between her mother and AJ. She tried to put on a happy face but felt the edges of her mouth turn down into a scowl when she caught her sister's gaze.

"Thank you for letting me stay and share dinner with your family," Savannah said once everyone was seated.

"You were like family in college. Of course you're staying. And don't even think about going home tonight. We'll make up the spare bedroom for you," Jillian said.

They didn't bother with grace. They were never an overly religious family as it was. Daniel worked skillfully at carving up the turkey. Working in a butcher shop as a teenager had been a blessing, at least for Thanksgiving and Christmas dinner. With plates piled high, everyone fell silent, focusing on the food in front of them.

Several hours later, Kalina's mother retired to one of the third-floor rooms. The nice part about having a three-story house was all the extra rooms. Kalina flaked out on the couch in the living room in a bit of a haze. Her head throbbed from too much wine and she knew she should probably lie down in bed but she was too comfortable to move. She was vaguely aware of someone pulling a blanket over her and footsteps on the stairs but didn't register specific people. The storm continued to rage outside, lulling her to sleep. Sometime later, she woke with start at the sound of something rumbling. Disoriented and still half-asleep, she looked around for the source of the noise but couldn't find it. A bright light passed through the front window, making shadows on the living room floor, but it was gone almost as quickly as it came. With a sigh, she curled up beneath the blanket and drifted back to sleep.

3

Sunlight streamed through the front window of the living room, rousing Kalina from her half-asleep state. She sat up, rubbed her eyes and looked around the living room, remembering she'd fallen asleep on the couch. She untangled her legs from the blanket and headed upstairs to brush her teeth and wash her face. She hadn't intended to spend the night and had no other clothes to change into. She wasn't about to borrow something from her sister's closet. After doing what she could to make herself presentable, she headed back downstairs and made a bee-line for the coffee pot. Her brother-in-law stood in front of it.

"Mind pouring me a cup?" she asked.

Daniel jumped and a plate clattered to the counter, revealing the remnants of some of her applesauce cake. He blushed bright red and she couldn't help but giggle.

"I won't tell Jillian," she said and brushed some crumbs from the front of his shirt.

"Thanks." The color receded a little as he reached for a mug and delivered the requested beverage.

Kalina savored the coffee, letting the caffeine wake up her senses. She peered out the kitchen window into the backyard. To her surprise the few trees in the yard hadn't lost any branches. "That was one crazy storm yesterday," she said.

"Yeah. It was." He set his plate in the sink and ran water over it, getting rid of the evidence of his non-traditional breakfast. "You know, I heard what you said to Jillian last night about AJ working at the shop."

Kalina choked on the sip of coffee she'd just taken. "Oh."

"I agree with you. She can't just pull him away from work whenever she feels like it. But what she probably wouldn't tell you is that she's been having a hard time letting him go and grow up. I mean he's got his learner's permit now and he's becoming more independent. I think she's just scared about him being out in the real world on his own in a couple of years."

"I get that but when I'm at work I have to treat him like an employee, not my nephew."

"Believe me, I understand."

Kalina caught sight of the clock on the microwave and nearly spit in her mug. "Is that the time?"

Daniel glanced over his shoulder. "It's not even eight yet."

"It's Black Friday."

"Oh, big comic buying day, is it?"

"Big retail day period."

Daniel laughed, lips spreading wide to reveal a straight, white smile. "I'm only kidding. If you need to head out, go for it. I'll give your best to Jill and AJ and Mom."

"I could actually use AJ's help."

Her brother-in-law looked toward the staircase. "If you can drag his butt out of bed, be my guest."

"Oh, and tell Jill I'll meet her at the station when I can get a break. I want to be there when Savannah reports her husband missing."

"Any particular reason?"

She pursed her lips. "I just want to make sure she gets all the important information to whoever takes the report."

"In other words, in case it isn't Chris, you want to make sure the boys in blue don't screw up."

Kalina held a finger to her lips. "Something like that."

Draining the coffee mug, she set it in the sink and headed upstairs to rouse her nephew. She knocked twice on his bedroom door before sticking her head in. The person-shaped lump beneath the covers signaled he was still in dreamland.

"Hey, you need to get up. I need you down at the shop."

He moaned and poked his head out from beneath the blankets. "Do you know what time it is?"

"I do. Now get moving, kiddo. You're on the clock in a half hour. Don't be late."

AJ pulled the blankets back over his head. Kalina turned to head back down to find her car keys and nearly knocked Savannah down the stairs. "So sorry!" she apologized.

Savannah managed to regain her footing and rubbed at her eyes. They were red-rimmed as if she'd been crying again. "So you really think I should go to the police?"

"Yes. I'd like to go with you. I know the lead detective in the department and I can make sure he takes the case."

"That's so nice of you. You really don't have to help me."

"Don't be ridiculous. My sister treats you like family, so you are family. I'll meet you two down at the station around eleven."

"Thank you." Savannah pulled Kalina into an awkward one-armed hug.

Kalina wiggled out of the hug as best she could and took the stairs two at a time. Daniel stood at the bottom of the stairs, holding her coat out for her.

"What a gentleman," she said and slipped it on.

"I'll make sure AJ's at work on time," he said as she fished her keys out of her coat pocket.

She was halfway out the door when

Daniel caught her wrist and shoved her phone into her outstretched hand. She flashed him a smile before heading out. She needed to stop by her apartment and clean up before she headed into work. It would also give her time to give Chris a call and see how he was. She didn't want to be angry with him and she figured it was a good idea to give him a heads up that they were coming in so someone would be around to take the missing person report. Once she'd maneuvered her car around the others parked in the driveway and was on the road, she gave Chris a call, making sure to put it on speaker phone. It rang three times before he picked up.

"Hello?" He sounded exhausted.

"Hey, I just wanted to check in and see how you were," she said.

"It was a long night. I just got in a couple hours ago."

"Jeez. It was that bad?"

"Getting techs out in the storm was tough.

Look, I'll make it up to you about last night."

"Don't worry about it. You didn't miss much."

"But you made my favorite dessert."

She grinned at herself in the rearview mirror. "I'll make some for you."

"You're the best." He yawned on the other end of the line.

"Look, I just wanted to ask who is working at the precinct today."

"Should I be worried?"

"No, not really. I just had to refer someone to the police to file a report and I wanted to make sure there were actually bodies at the station today given all the craziness yesterday."

"Yeah. Someone will be there."

"Great. Look, go back to sleep. I'll see you later. I love you."

"Love you too."

The line went dead and her phone hung up the call on its own. She pulled into the driveway of her building and raced inside to grab a quick shower. Feeling refreshed and ready to face the day, she climbed back behind the steering wheel and made the short journey to Geeks and Things. There was already a line of beleaguered adults accompanying young kids all eager to pick up their Black Friday swag. She unlocked the back door just as her nephew rolled up on his bike. He still looked half-asleep.

"Perk up, kiddo. You play your cards right and you'll get a bonus out of this," she said with a smirk.

"Black Friday is evil," he mumbled and followed her inside.

Kalina flipped on the lights in the game room and the front of the store and booted up the tablet so it was ready for transactions. AJ unlocked the cash drawer for the likely onslaught of cash purchases—kids saved up all of their allowance for days like today—and did a quick cash count.

"I think we're ready," he said, appearing to wake up a little more as the silhouettes of eager customers shifted outside the front door.

Kalina put on a big smile and said, "Let's do this thing!"

The next three hours were a blur of giddy yelps of excitement as kids bought her wares for the first time with their own, carefully saved up, money. She had some usual customers come in for their weekly orders and some new, curious faces drop by thanks to the holiday weekend. Some of the adults shooed the children accompanying them into the game room while they attempted to do some covert Christmas shopping outside the view of prying eyes.

"Thanks so much for shopping at Geeks and Things. We hope to see you again for all your nerdy needs," Kalina called as the last customer walked out.

She collapsed against the counter and

glanced at AJ. He looked wide awake and a bit shell shocked. He eased the cash drawer shut and slumped on to the stool behind the counter. "That was insane, Aunt K."

"There might still be more. And I need you to hold things down for me for a little while."

He let out a whine. "Where are you going?"

"I promised your mom and Savannah I'd go with them to the precinct so Savannah can file a missing person report."

"Oh, right. Do you think he is really missing?"

"No idea. People don't come home for lots of reasons. Not all of them are the worst case scenario."

"Don't worry about the shop. I got it covered."

She reached over and ruffled his hair before she went in search of her coat and keys. Just as she climbed in behind the wheel, her phone buzzed with an incoming call from Jillian. "Hey, I'm heading over to the precinct now."

"Oh, good. I guess we'll see you there. Now, you're sure someone will be there?"

"Yes. See you in a few minutes."

Tossing the phone onto the passenger seat, Kalina started the car and made a U-turn out of the parking lot. As she got situated back on Main Street, she saw a few more people wandering in the direction of the shop. She sent off a silent 'good luck' to her nephew. He was a smart kid and could handle the shop for a little while. She assumed she would be back by lunchtime and she could take over so he could eat. A couple minutes later, she found a spot in the parking lot outside the precinct and spotted her sister's car two spots over.

"Ready?" she asked Savannah once they all stood at the front door.

"No, but I don't have a choice."

4

____

Kalina trailed the other two women as they walked in and stopped at the reception desk. Jimmy sat there with a distant look in his eyes. Kalina knew he'd been on the scene with Chris most of the night. What was he doing there now?

"Hey, Jimmy. I'm surprised to see you here," Kalina said, taking control of the situation.

He yawned, barely stifling it. "When the boss says to pull a double, you do it."

They still didn't have a new Chief of Police and Chris seemed adamant about not taking the position. Kalina didn't entirely get why, since he was a good cop and everyone looked to him for guidance anyway. If they wanted to keep things in-house after the debacle of Captain Cahill, he was the logical choice.

"I heard yesterday was rough." She gave him a sympathetic smile. "The reason we're here though is a friend of ours needs to file a missing person report. You can help her with that, right?"

Jimmy looked to Savannah who gave him a plaintive look and tugged at her hair. Oh, yeah, he was definitely paying attention now. He scrambled from behind the desk and ushered them toward the bull pen and an empty desk. He dutifully pulled out a chair for Savannah to sit in before he booted up the computer. Jillian pulled over a chair from a nearby desk and settled in beside her friend. Kalina remained standing over Savannah's right shoulder and looked around. Chris was probably still sleeping. Or maybe he was down at the crime scene. Speaking of which, she spotted some photos of a man taped to a whiteboard with 'John Doe' scrawled across the top. It was bloated and waterlogged but she could swear he looked familiar.

"Okay, now Miss... " Jimmy trailed off, waiting for Savannah to fill in the rest.

"Mrs. Chase. I... I would like to report someone missing."

"And who would that be?"

"My husband. Thomas Chase."

Jimmy hastily jotted down notes on a pad in front of him. Kalina tuned out of the conversation for a minute, focusing on the board across the room. She'd met Mr. Chase only once—when her friend Nadine sold her family home—but she remembered him well, with thinning, grey-brown hair and sincere, green eyes. She couldn't verify eye color but the hair on John Doe looked right.

She leaned over to whisper in Jillian's ear. "Take a look at that photo on the board over there. Does he look familiar to you?"

Savannah stopped mid-sentence—having heard Kalina's question—and turned to look at her. She got up from her seat and inched closer, studying the picture. Her body language changed almost instantly. Kalina raced forward when Savannah started to sway and guided her back to the chair. Jillian had turned pale.

"Is something wrong, Mrs. Chase?" Jimmy asked. Poor guy wasn't exactly the world's most perceptive investigator.

"Why ... why is there a photo of my husband on that board?"

Jimmy cleared his throat, opened his mouth and closed it again. "Um ... you're sure that's your husband?"

"Yes. We've been married for three years. I think I'd know the man I share a bed with."

Jimmy looked to Kalina as if she held the

answers to his questions but she shook her head and gestured to her phone. She mouthed 'Chris' and his cheeks flushed. He took a deep breath and picked up the receiver. "I'm going to call Detective Harper. He should really talk to you about this."

5

———

Jillian went in search of tissues for Savannah while Jimmy made the call to Chris. Kalina stayed standing, observing the whole situation with a growing sense of unease. A million questions flooded her thoughts. Namely, how had Thomas Chase ended up dead in the last day? At least his death explained why he hadn't gone home the day before Thanksgiving. Jimmy tapped his fingers nervously against the desk while he waited for Chris to answer the call.

"Detective Harper, it's Jimmy. I need you to get down to the station right away. We've got an ID on the"—he glanced over at Kalina —"case from yesterday." He paused. "His wife came in to report him missing."

He nodded his head as Chris said something on the other end of the line. Jillian returned and handed a wad of crumpled napkins from the kitchen area to Savannah. She wiped at her eyes and sniffled loudly while Jimmy wrapped up the call. Finally, he set the receiver back in the cradle and cleared his throat again.

"Detective Harper will be down shortly to speak with you about your husband. I'm sorry for your loss, ma'am."

Kalina felt bad for Jimmy. He'd no doubt never had to notify anyone about the death of a loved one before. The only other big cases he'd been involved with had victims who didn't have any living relatives or were already aware of the crime. Thinking back on those cases, Kalina wondered how Nadine was faring. They'd talked and emailed around Halloween and she'd been settling in but the family holidays were probably still rough for her.

"Can I ask ... where he was found? And what happened?" Savannah asked between sniffles.

"It's probably better if you just wait for the detective. I'm not really handling the case."

An awkward silence fell over the station. Jimmy stood up and hurried back to the front desk, leaving the grieving widow in the care of Jillian and Kalina. For her part, Jillian made soft shushing noises and wrapped her friend in a wordless hug. Kalina moved away, wanting to give them privacy, and she approached the front desk.

"You okay? You look a little freaked out."

"I've never had to tell someone their husband was dead."

"It's part of the job, right? They train you for it."

"I know. I just feel so bad for her. This is supposed to be a time that's all about family and being thankful and now she's got to bury the man she loves."

"I'm sure you could help ease her mind if you shared just a couple details. Nothing gruesome. But maybe if he was alone when it happened?" Sure, she wanted the details herself but she wanted Jimmy to be able to handle things on his own as a cop. Chris wouldn't always be around to steer him.

He stood up straighter and pivoted to head back to the desk where Savannah and Jillian sat huddled together. He'd only a few steps before the front doors opened and Chris rushed in looking disheveled. His shirt wasn't tucked in and his hair was more bed-head than naturally tussled. Kalina motioned for

Jimmy to continue his task and she spun to stop Chris before he got too far.

"You want to fill me in?" he asked as she smoothed down his hair and straightened his shirt.

"Savannah Chase. Wife of Thomas Chase. He's a real estate broker I think. She ended up at my sister's house yesterday because she hadn't seen her husband in a day and she was worried."

"Why'd she go to your sister?"

"They're college friends. I convinced her to come in and report him missing. Looks like there's a reason he didn't come home."

"Thanks." He gave her a quick kiss before stepping around her and sidling up to the group.

Suspecting the conversation would be longer than the previous one, Kalina grabbed an empty chair and pulled it up. Chris didn't even comment on her and Jillian's continued presence during the interview. He retrieved a

notepad and pen from his own desk and settled in.

"Mrs. Chase, I'm very sorry to have to in-
form you that your husband was found last
night."

"Where was he? What happened?"

"He was in an abandoned property down
by the beach. He'd been shot."

Savannah devolved into another fit of hys-
terics and rocked back and forth. Jimmy visibly
recoiled at the emotional outburst. Chris sat pa-
tiently, pen at the ready to jot down notes. Kalina
had to admit she liked watching him work.

"I'm sorry," Savannah mumbled into the
wad of damp napkins. "I don't understand
who would want to hurt him."

"Remind me what your husband did for a
living."

"He was a real estate broker in town.
Everyone liked him. He'd never hurt a fly.
Please, do you have any suspects?"

"We're still investigating. It would help us establish a better timeline if you could give us some information about the last time you saw him."

"It was the day before Thanksgiving. He went into work like he always does. He didn't come home at the normal time but that's not unusual. He'll always call me and tell me if he's running late so I don't worry."

"Did your husband call you that night?"

"No. Which is why I started to get concerned. He always called."

Chris scribbled something on the pad and looked up. "How often would your husband work late?"

"What?"

"Out of a month, how many nights do you think he worked late?"

"A few. I don't really remember."

"Can you try to think a little harder?"

"I guess maybe five or six times a month. It

didn't seem that frequent. Why? Is that important?"

Chris cleared his throat and pursed his lips. Kalina could tell he was choosing his next words carefully. "Is it possible your husband wasn't working late those nights?"

The color in Savannah's cheeks drained. "Are you accusing my husband of cheating on me?"

"I can't imagine there was much reason for a real estate broker to work late that often."

"He'd never cheat on me." Savannah's cheeks burned bright red and her shoulders stiffened. Chris had clearly hit a nerve.

"I don't mean to sound insensitive but you aren't Mr. Chase's first wife," Chris said.

Kalina shot Jillian a confused look. There'd been another Mrs. Chase? Clearly, being away from town during college and afterwards had done her more of a disservice in being in the know on town gossip than she'd realized.

"That isn't fair, Detective," Jillian interrupted.

"His first wife died of breast cancer six years ago. It took him a really long time to get over her," Savannah said, her tone much quieter now.

Kalina tried to hide the shock on her face but quickly realized no one was really paying her any attention. Chris looked down at the notes he'd taken and then back up at Savannah.

"I wasn't implying anything negative about his first wife. But ... it is a little suspicious that a woman such as yourself would be interested in a man like Thomas."

"What's that supposed to mean?"

"You're quite a bit younger than he was."

Savannah leapt from her chair, her hands balled into fists, and shouted, "Are you calling me a gold digger?"

Chris didn't appear fazed. "No. I'm merely stating that it might seem strange to some

people that there was such a big age difference."

"We were in love."

Jillian tugged on Savannah's arm until the blonde woman sat back down. Her facial features stormed with anger and insult. If Chris had struck a nerve with the implication that Thomas had cheated on her, she was livid with the accusation that she'd only married him for his money.

"I don't appreciate you dragging me or my husband through the mud like this, Detective. I want to know what you're doing to find out who did this to him!"

"I apologize, Mrs. Chase. I didn't mean to upset you. I can assure you we are looking into every lead we can. Was your husband selling any beach-front property that you knew of? Maybe he was meeting a client later in the day out there?"

"He didn't talk about his work much."

"So you didn't know which properties he

was currently trying to sell?"

"No. I'm sorry. Not that I can think of anyway."

Chris tapped his pen against his notepad and stared intently at it. Kalina could tell he was weighing the best option on how to move forward. By the way his shoulders tightened and he leaned forward, she guessed he wanted to continue to question Savannah. But she appeared to be closing herself off.

"Mrs. Chase, I'm going to need you to go to the morgue and make an identification just so we can be absolutely sure it's your husband. Do you think you can do that?"

Savannah let out a couple more sniffles and dabbed at her eyes. "I think so. Can Jillian go with me?"

"Sure. I'll have Jimmy go with you." He waved to get Jimmy's attention.

Jimmy pulled on his jacket and waited for Jillian and Savannah to stand up and gather themselves. Kalina stayed seated, as did Chris.

He scribbled down a few more notes before spinning around his chair.

"Mrs. Chase, just one last question."

She stopped and looked over her shoulder. "Yes?"

"What company did your husband work for?"

"Eastern Seaboard Realty."

"Thanks."

6
____

Chris blew out a breath as soon as they were alone. Kalina scooted her chair over and took his hand in hers, hoping it would help alleviate some of the stress keeping his jaw and shoulders tight.

"That went ... sort of well," she offered with a one-shouldered shrug.

"If it really is her husband, I feel sorry for her."

"Do you really think someone would want to kill him? A client or something?"

"I don't know. Maybe. I mean real estate can be rather competitive."

"I met him once. A couple months ago when Nadine was selling her place. He seemed nice enough and she was happy with the money she got from working with him."

"What's your take on Mrs. Chase?"

Kalina arched a brow. "What do you mean?"

"Do you find her credible?"

"If you mean do I think she's really upset that her husband is dead then yeah. I'd say she's credible. Other than that, I only met her last night. All we talked about was her husband being missing. Dinner wasn't exactly full of conversation."

"Everything all right?"

Kalina let out a sigh. "It was just an argument with Jill about AJ working at the shop this weekend. It will get sorted out."

"Speaking of which, isn't today a big sales day for you guys?"

"Yeah. I left AJ in charge." She glanced at the time. "I should get back. I promised him I'd only be gone an hour."

"I might bring my nephews by a little later."

"I'll look forward to it. And I hope things work out with this case and you get a lead." She kissed him for longer than strictly necessary. He didn't seem to mind in the least.

She retrieved her phone and sent off a text to her nephew, assuring him she'd be there in a few minutes so he could take lunch. She hoped the lunch rush wouldn't be too bad because she had a little research she wanted to do on Eastern Seaboard Realty.

Five minutes later, she pulled in behind the shop. There weren't hordes of people beating down the doors so maybe she'd get lucky and have some peace and quiet. AJ greeted her at the back door—another sign things weren't too busy—and grinned at her.

"Things went awesome while you were

gone. We made a bunch of sales. I even convinced some people to get more than they came in for."

"Good job. I'll take over for a while."

"I could stay if you want. Just in case."

She pushed past him into the game room and headed to the front of the store. He trailed behind her like an eager puppy.

"I think you should take a little time off," she said without looking at him.

"Why? I thought I was doing well?"

"You are. You're been a great help."

"So what's the problem?"

She turned to face him. "This isn't a punishment, okay? Your mom and dad told me last night that your mom's been having a hard time with you being away from the house so much."

"So she put you up to this?"

Kalina kneaded her temples. "You are growing up so fast and before you know it you'll be out in the world at college and living your own life as an adult. Your mom isn't ready to let you go just yet. I think she just wants to spend a little time with you. That's all this is. I promise."

Her nephew pouted and his shoulders fell as if he'd been scolded. He looked so much younger than his sixteen years in that moment and she had to resist the urge to wrap him in a tight, comforting embrace. Here, she was his boss not his aunt. Hugging an employee would be totally inappropriate.

"It's only for a couple days," she said and tried to give him a reassuring smile.

He rolled his eyes and made his way back through the game room. The back door slammed shut and Kalina let out a sigh of frustration. Why did teenage boys have to be so moody? She settled in behind the front counter and checked the transaction log on the tablet and did a quick cash count just to be sure everything looked right. She had to admit she was impressed with the number of sales. She made a mental note to compare next year to see if the holiday weekend was consistent.

Satisfied that the books were temporarily settled, Kalina pulled up the browser on the tablet and easily found the contact information for the realty company. According to the contact page, the company's main office was not far from the waterfront where Thomas had been found. After deciding to play the part of a prospective client, she entered the number into her phone and hit 'Call'.

After four rings, a bored sounding woman's voice answered, "Eastern Seaboard Realty. How can I help you?"

Kalina put on her bubbliest voice possible. "Oh, hi, I was hoping to speak with one of your realtors about listing my house for sale."

"Hold for a moment."

The line turned to static as Kalina was put on hold. She pulled the phone from her ear to check that the connection was still good. The timer on the call continued to tick off the seconds. She started kicking her heel against the bottom of the stool while she waited for the woman to come back on the line.

"I'm sorry, all of our realtors have full client lists."

"Are you sure? A friend of mine referred me. She said the realtor she had was great. Thomas Chase was his name."

"He doesn't work here anymore." Her tone shifted, taking on an edge.

"Are you sure? She only worked with him a couple months ago."

"Yes. I'm sorry but we can't help you." The line went dead and this time the timer stopped and ended the call.

Kalina stared at her phone in confused silence. Her little experiment had only yielded more questions. Did Savannah know her husband was no longer working for the real estate company? When did he stop working there and where had he been going all this time? More importantly, why couldn't the firm help her even if Thomas was no longer an employee? There was definitely something off about the whole situation. Before she could decide what to do next, her phone screen lit up with a call from her sister.

"Hey, I wanted to let you know that I gave AJ the weekend off."

"Oh, thanks." She was clearly distracted.

"How did it go at the morgue?"

"It's him. It was so awful seeing him lying there like that."

"Tell Savannah I'm so sorry."

"Yeah. Look, I need Detective Harper's direct number. Can you send it to me?"

"Sure. Why, what's going on?"

"Someone vandalized the Chases' house. Broke and smashed up a bunch of stuff."

"Oh, God, is everyone okay?"

"We think it happened while Savannah's been with us."

"I'll get you Chris's number right now."

"Thanks."

7

───────────

Kalina let the phone fall from her fingers and clatter to the countertop. What would make someone want to vandalize the Chases' house? Maybe whoever shot Thomas had been watching the house and did it after Savannah left the night before. Something about the timing piqued her curiosity and she flipped the front door sign to 'Closed' and headed out again. If Chris asked why she was at the new crime scene, she could reasonably say she was there to support her sister and friend. She also wanted to tell him about Thomas no longer being employed at the real estate firm.

She had to look at the address online before she headed out. It turned out that the Chases lived in a not-so-modest, three-story, sprawling house near the beach. It was set far enough back that high tides wouldn't cause trouble but close enough that they could still claim they had beach-front property. The flashing lights of the police cruiser nearly blinded her as she pulled up and parked one house over. Crime scene technicians were already flitting in and out of the house with evidence bags and fingerprint powder. Savannah huddled with Jillian off to the side, talking to Chris. Kalina climbed out of her car and got within earshot long enough to hear the gist. According to Savannah, the house had been fine when she left on Thanksgiving and she hadn't been back until then so that had to be the window of opportunity.

"Once the techs are done, I'd like to do a walk through with you, just so we can have an accurate inventory of anything that might be missing," Chris said and Savannah nodded.

There was something off about the front door. Trying not to look too obvious, Kalina made her way over so she had a clear view. Someone had spray painted the word 'Traitor' on the front door. Traitor of what? To whom? This only made things more complicated. She really needed to share with Chris what she'd found about Thomas's employment situation but she wouldn't just horn in on his conversation with a grieving widow. In her peripheral vision, she spotted a man dressed in a dark suit and tie standing at the end of the road, observing the scene. Immediately, the tiny hairs on the back of her neck stood on end, signaling he didn't belong. Abruptly, the man turned and strode off, hands in his pockets. Kalina discreetly followed him until he stopped halfway up the beach at a sign for Carlisle Premiere Developments.

"Excuse me, sir!" The words were out of her mouth before she realized she'd spoken.

The man stopped and waited for her to catch up and spun on his heel to face her. Up close he was imposing with a sharp jaw and linebacker shoulders. He pressed his lips into a thin line of displeasure at his day being interrupted by a silly comic shop owner playing detective.

"Yes?" His voice was high and nasally, not at all what Kalina expected to come out of such a large man.

"You don't happen to work for the development company do you?"

Instead of answering, he reached into his breast pocket and produced a business card. She took it and glanced over the text. The mystery man was Victor Mackland, Asset Protection Manager. Mr. Mackland did indeed work for the development company.

"I saw you down the street and I wanted to ask what you could tell me about what's happening here on the waterfront. I'm relatively new to town." She prayed he hadn't seen her on Main Street any time recently.

"The company is building a new hotel and some high end waterfront condos."

"Oh, wow. That sounds great. I mean it will just boost tourism to town and increase revenue. But ... what about the people who live here?"

"I'm sorry, Miss. If you have more questions, you'll need to speak to one of our girls in sales. Good day."

Before she could say more, Mr. Mackland did an about face and strode off out of sight. Kalina stayed put for a minute trying to process the new information. She needed to do a little fact checking to see if there really was a new development project happening and how Thomas Chase was involved. Shaking her head, she made her way back up the beach and the street to the Chase house. The technicians were loading up the last of their gear and Chris and Savannah had disappeared. Jillian stood alone by the front steps.

"This is getting pretty crazy," Kalina said and sidled up to her sister.

"Savannah is going to stay with us until this is all over. It clearly isn't safe for her to be here alone."

"That makes sense. Hey, do you know anything about a new hotel and condos going up on the beach?"

"Yeah, a lot of people weren't too happy when that contract came through."

"Why not?"

Jillian rolled her eyes. "Honestly, Kal. Read a newspaper sometime. Building the new hotel and condos means the people who live there now will have to give up their houses. And a lot of the older population of town live out there. They don't have anywhere to go. But the town agreed to the project so there's not much they can do."

"Thanks. I need to get back to the shop. Let me know if you need anything."

Her sister gave a weary smile and nodded. Time to do some more digging.

8

The trip back to the shop was short and she found AJ flipping through the Cards against Humanity deck at the front counter. She set her phone down on the counter beside him and scooted him out of the way.

"Things seem to have slowed down," he said.

"That's how it usually is."

"Sorry I got mad at you before, Aunt K."

"Don't worry about it."

"So what's the latest news on our dead guy?"

"Well, he hasn't worked for the real estate firm in at least two months and there was a man from Carlisle Premiere Developments lurking around the Chase house after it had been vandalized. That was kind of suspicious."

"Oh, they're the guys who are building the luxury hotel on the waterfront."

"So I'm told. But something seems off. I can't really explain it."

"You know who you remind me of?" her nephew said.

"Who?"

"Jessica Jones."

She smacked his arm. "I am not."

"You help people without being asked and you are pretty awesome. Plus you own your own business."

"I'm also not a super powered drunk."

"She's got charm."

"Yeah, OK. Look, I need to see what I can find out about this company so I'm going to be in the back if you want to hang out here."

"Absolutely."

Kalina grabbed the tablet from beside the register and headed to one of the big, comfy chairs in the corner. She could still keep an eye on the store and dig up some dirt on the development company. Needing to concentrate, she put in her earbuds and turned on some instrumental music. With the world effectively drowned out, she did a quick search for Carlisle Premiere Developments. Her search brought up a minimalist website with a contact number and some flashy photos of upscale developments. So at least the company was real. Navigating through the menu at the top of the page, she found a list of affiliate companies. She didn't have to look far to spot Eastern Seaboard Realty. Had Thomas Chase jumped ship from brokering real estate deals to developing high-end luxury hotels and condos? The change didn't make much sense to her but her gut told her there was something to this connection.

"Hey, AJ," she called, tugging one earbud from her ear.

Her nephew materialized in the doorway between the front of the store and the game room. "Yeah, Aunt K., what's up?"

"How did you hear about the hotel development going up on the waterfront again?"

"It was in the paper and, as I said, a lot of people weren't too happy about it going up."

"When did all this start? I mean I know I was away for a while but the fact they are moving forward feels kind of sudden."

"Uh, maybe over the summer. Well, I know Mom and Dad went to some town meetings back in January or February—before Grandpa died—about using the land for the new development. I think they only finalized the deal in like September. Why?"

"It might be relevant to the case. Apparently, Mr. Chase doesn't work for the real estate firm anymore. I know he did in late September or early October because he helped Nadine sell her house but I called earlier and they said he doesn't work there anymore."

"So?"

She handed over the tablet. "His firm is an affiliate company with the developer. I'm thinking maybe he went to go work for them. I'd imagine it paid better I just don't know what a real estate broker would be doing at a development firm."

"Maybe call and ask them? It can't hurt, right?"

"I'm not so sure about that. Remember, the development firm had some Asset Protection manager lurking around while the police were investigating the break-in. When I tried to ask him questions, he blew me off and walked away."

"Weird. Does Detective Harper know that

Mr. Chase left the company?"

"I don't know. I haven't told him yet but I know he was going to check into it."

"As I said, it can't hurt to call and see if they'll admit Mr. Chase worked for them. You can borrow my phone if you want."

Kalina gave her nephew a grateful smile but shook her head. "Your mother would kill me. I'll use mine."

She pulled the earbuds from the headphone jack and dialed the company's main number. It rang twice before a chipper-sounding woman answered.

"Carlisle Premiere Developments, how may I help you today?"

Kalina let out a breath. "Hi. I might have the wrong number but I'm trying to reach Thomas Chase."

"One moment please." Static filled the other end of the line. "I'm sorry, he's not in today and I'm not sure when he'll be back in. I can leave a message for you if you'd like."

"No, that's all right but thanks so much. You have a good day now."

Kalina stared dumbstruck at her nephew as she ended the call. "Remind me to give you a raise. You are a smart kid. He definitely worked there before … he died." She managed to catch herself before she said murdered. Sure, it was accurate but it sounded overly gruesome.

"If only we could talk to his boss at the old place, maybe find out why he left."

"There's no 'we' here. But I might be able to drop a hint or two. Thanks kiddo."

"I'm here all week. And by the way, you are *totally* Jessica Jones."

The bell above the door jingled, signaling a new customer, and Kalina shooed AJ back to front desk duty. She had plenty of reasons to drop into the police station without Chris becoming suspicious of her motives. Besides, he owed her for missing Thanksgiving with her family.

Kalina waited until after 6:30 to grab some pizza and head over to the station. She'd picked up a couple extra slices in case Jimmy was around. He tended to horn in on their office dinners, even if he didn't mean to. She found Chris hunched over his computer staring at some file or other.

"Hey, I brought food," she announced.

He looked up and smiled. The bags under his eyes were more pronounced than they'd been that morning and he looked paler. "Thanks."

She settled in beside him and handed over a big slice of Hawaiian and a napkin. It was half gone with two bites. She nibbled on a slice of sausage and green pepper. They ate in companionable silence for a few minutes before she set her food down and looked at him.

"I know you can't say much but how is Savannah doing?"

"She seems to be holding up. She's going through hell though. First her husband is killed and then her house is ripped apart."

"Did she know what they were looking for?"

"She claims to have no idea."

"But you don't believe her?"

"It just seems odd that a real estate broker would be the target of these kinds of crimes. Especially in this town. Despite the few incidents recently, we aren't a high crime area."

"He isn't working for the firm anymore."

Chris propped his elbow on the arm of the chair and stared at her. "And you know this how?"

Kalina studied her hands. "I called and asked for him and they said he didn't work there anymore."

"I guess I would have found that out anyhow tonight."

"Oh?"

"Mr. Chase's ... former boss is coming in for questioning in about an hour."

"That's late isn't it?" She took a bite of pizza.

"It fit with his schedule."

Kalina nodded. "There's more."

"Of course there is."

"There was a guy from the development company looking around and when I called and asked for Mr. Chase, the secretary told me he was out. That all but confirms he worked there. And the real estate firm is an affiliate of the developer. It says so right on their website."

"That's definitely strange." A new message bubble popped up on Chris's computer screen. He turned to study it, his brow knitting together in concern. "That's not good."

Kalina leaned forward to try to read over his shoulder. "What is it?"

"I just got information back on the gun we found at the scene. It was registered to Mr. Chase."

"And I'm betting Mrs. Chase doesn't know he had a gun."

"I'm thinking not." He rubbed the back of his neck—a telltale sign of stress and frustration—and blew out a breath. "Honestly, none of this makes sense."

She rubbed his back gently to help ease some of the tension. "I'm sure it will."

Two sets of footsteps echoed on the linoleum behind them, drawing Kalina's attention. Jimmy—her go to for inside information—walked by the front desk, accompanied by a man in a navy suit. He was balding with sparse hair left on the sides. It could have been brown at one point but it was grey now.

"Sorry to interrupt, boss, but Mr. Linden is here to see you," Jimmy announced. He eyed the extra slice of Hawaiian pizza on Chris's desk.

Chris spun around and took in the realtor before him. Without a word, Kalina grabbed an extra napkin to go with the pizza and offered Mr. Linden her chair. She and Jimmy retreated a safe distance—still within earshot—before she handed over the pizza.

"You didn't have to," he said before taking a big bite.

"You guys work too hard," she said.

Mr. Linden settled into the chair Kalina had vacated while Chris hastily cleared away the pizza remains and retrieved his pen and notepad. Kalina couldn't keep from smiling at how he clung to old school traditions. It only made her love him more.

"Thanks for coming down, Mr. Linden. I appreciate it."

Mr. Linden shrugged one shoulder. "Not sure what I can tell you. Thomas Chase is no longer an employee with our firm."

"So I hear. Can you describe what happened?"

"Nothing to say really. Decided he wasn't interested in selling homes anymore and quit."

"So you didn't have any concerns about his performance?"

"None. He was a good worker. One of our best in fact. It was a shame to see him leave."

"Were you aware of anything going on in his home life that might have prompted a change?"

"Like what?"

"Anything. I know that Savannah Chase is his second wife."

"As far as I know, things were fine between them. He didn't talk about her much. Just between us, I thought it was a little strange he married again. They just don't seem compatible."

Chris tapped the capped end of the pen against his lower lip. "Did you know Mr. Chase was employed by Carlisle Premiere Developments?"

"No I didn't know that."

"Does that surprise you?"

"A little." Mr. Linden's cheeks paled.

Even from where Kalina stood, she could see sweat break out on his temple. Chris clearly noted the change too.

"Do you have any idea what sort of work Mr. Chase would be doing for a development company?"

Mr. Linden coughed and averted his gaze. "Can't say that I do. You'd be better off asking them."

"Oh, I will be. Is there anything else you

can tell me about Mr. Chase? Can you think of anyone who would have wanted to hurt him?"

"No idea. I'm sorry. If that's all, I need to be going."

Chris offered his hand and Mr. Linden shook it. "Thank you again for coming down."

Mr. Linden stood, straightened his suit jacket and strode out of the station without a word to anyone else. The interview had been somewhat illuminating but Kalina realized it was time to talk to Savannah again. She couldn't believe she hadn't noticed her husband change careers. And she couldn't get the image of the developer goon out of her head.

"Hey, Jimmy, can you tell Chris I'll see him tomorrow? I need to go check in with my sister to make sure everything is going all right at her house."

"Sure thing, Kal."

10

———

Kalina texted AJ to let him know he should close up the shop for the night. She'd swing by afterwards to double check the register and handle the books for the day. The lights were on in the living room of her sister's house when she pulled into the driveway. She pulled in behind Daniel's car and took the front steps two at a time. She didn't bother knocking, instead choosing to make a bold entrance. She found her sister and Savannah sharing a bottle of wine in the living room.

"You know doors are meant for knocking, right?" Jillian said before proffering a third glass.

Kalina waved dismissively at the offered glass. "I just figured you'd want to hear what I have to say."

"Is it about Thomas?" Savannah's cheeks were flushed from the alcohol.

"Yes. I was having dinner with Chris and he told me that Thomas left the real estate firm a few months ago and was working for the developers who are putting up the hotel and condos on the waterfront."

"That's ridiculous," Jillian scoffed.

Savannah's cheeks flushed more and her eyes grew bright with unshed tears. "I feel awful."

"Why?" Kalina sat down on the couch beside the woman.

"I just remembered that he had left the

firm. I didn't realize he didn't work for the same type of company anymore. Oh God, am I going to get into trouble with the police?"

"Of course not," Jillian interjected, shooting Kalina a look that clearly said 'she better not get in trouble'.

"I think if you just sit down with Detective Harper and tell him whatever you've remembered, he'll understand. After all, you've had quite a shock the last couple days."

Savannah nodded and rubbed at her nose with her free hand. The tension in the room eased a little but Kalina was still on edge. She needed to probe a little more about some of the other information she'd gathered.

"There's something else that Detective Harper found."

"What now?"

"The gun that was found with Thomas's body ... the one used to shoot him was registered to him."

"That isn't possible. He didn't keep weapons in the house. Thomas hated guns."

Kalina leaned in a little closer. "Did you have a gun?"

"God, no!" The wine glass slipped through her fingers and smashed against the coffee table, spraying the carpet with red wine and glass shards.

Jillian jumped into action, rushing out of the room and returning moments later with a dustpan and brush to sweep up the shards. She glared at Kalina but Kalina stayed put. Savannah curled into herself on the couch and dabbed at her eyes.

"You could help," Jillian snapped.

Just as Kalina opened her mouth to fire back at her sister, her phone buzzed with an incoming call from AJ. He must still have been at the shop. Without excusing herself, she stood up and left the living room.

"Hey, you should be home soon, right?"

"Yeah I'm on the way but I wanted to tell you something."

"OK. What is it?"

"I did what you'd do and did some newspaper digging. There was an article back in the summer about the fear that the property would displace people in the area. And I have a friend, Adrien Parker and his family are moving because the bank foreclosed on their house. And get this ... when I mentioned Mr. Chase, Adrien got all pissed off. Said that was the guy who showed up and forced them to accept the foreclosure."

"Where do they live?"

"Um, not far from the waterfront."

"Thanks, AJ. You did great. Now get your butt home before your mother has a heart attack."

Her nephew hung up and Kalina studied the blank screen for a moment. Things were starting to make sense. She didn't know much about foreclosures and the like but she did know someone who did and she was going to pick their brain as soon as she could make an excuse to get out of the house. But first she needed one final answer from Savannah.

"Who was that?" Savannah asked as soon as Kalina walked back into the room.

"Oh, that was nothing. Just someone calling the shop's main number. It forwards to my cell. I actually need to get back but I wanted to ask you one last thing. Did you notice if any of your neighbors had been moving away or getting foreclosed on recently?"

"No. Why would you ask that?"

"Well, I was just wondering why someone would spray paint 'Traitor' on your front door, that's all. Sorry about the wine, Jill."

11

Kalina climbed back into her car and let out a sigh. If Thomas Chase was working for the developer and forcing people out of their homes so the hotel and condos could be built that would definitely brand him a traitor, especially to families living on the waterfront. And it might give someone a motive to want him dead. She didn't quite believe that Savannah didn't know that her husband had changed careers and had gone from selling people homes to ripping them away from families. She pulled out her phone and dialed the switchboard number for the police station.

"Ellesworth Police Department," Jimmy said on the other end of the line.

"Hey Jimmy, it's Kalina. I need a favor from you."

"Sure, what's up?"

"Do you know anything about debt collection and foreclosures?"

"Some. My brother Alex knows more."

His brother worked as a firefighter in town. A family of public servants. "Is he off shift today?"

"I think so. Why, what's going on?"

"I'm just curious about some things. With the big development going in on the waterfront I want to be more informed about how it's happening. Can you guys swing by Geeks and Things in say an hour?"

"I'll give him a call. Should I let Detective Harper know?"

"That's not necessary."

"If you're sure. I'll hopefully see you in an hour."

"Great, I appreciate it."

Tossing the phone on the passenger seat, Kalina headed back to the shop to make sure she was ready for her late-night visitors. A part of her felt bad leaving Chris out of this investigative mission but he had other things to worry about. Besides, he needed to get some sleep.

Waiting for their arrival gave Kalina time to settle the day's bookkeeping. The shop had done well in profits. Black Friday was officially a success. The bell above the front door jangled and she looked up to see Jimmy and Alex stride in side by side. Alex was older than Jimmy by at least six years and had a broader build.

"Thanks for coming over, guys. Why don't we grab a seat in the back?"

They settled around one of the tables strewn with pieces of Settlers of Catan. Jimmy fiddled with a few pieces while Alex sat with his arms crossed over his chest.

"So what do you want to know about debt collection?"

"How it works. Why someone might get involved in it." She pulled out a pen and notebook Chris had given her to take notes.

Alex rubbed his chin. "Well, you get into it for the money. See when the bank or a credit card company has a client who isn't paying their debts off, they sell the debt to a collector on the cheap. A five thousand dollar loan might get sold for one thousand. Then the collector goes to the debtor and offers to wipe the debt clean if they pay twenty-five hundred. The collector nets fifteen hundred of that for himself."

"And the bank or the credit card company doesn't get anything for it?"

He shook his head. "No. They get the money on the front end when they sell the debt package."

"So someone would have to actually have the money to buy the debt in the first place and then they make it back with collecting on the debts. Pretty lucrative if you don't mind ruining people's lives."

Kalina nodded as she scribbled down the example he'd given. It still didn't seem like a career a mild-mannered guy in his 60s would suddenly take on. It was also suspicious that Savannah wouldn't have known if her husband made a huge purchase.

"You know … we found a receipt for a money transfer in the study at the Chase house. Something like thirty thousand dollars," Jimmy said.

Kalina leaned forward, pen poised to write. "Who was it to?"

"Didn't say. Just had bank information on it."

Alex cleared his throat and eyed his younger brother. "I don't think you should be sharing details about an ongoing case, Jim."

"Right, of course. Just forget I mentioned that."

Kalina gave Jimmy a smile. "Don't worry about it. I appreciate you guys explaining the debt collection stuff though."

"That kind of life can be dangerous too. You try to collect from the wrong person and things could go sideways fast," Alex said and stood up.

"That's what I'm afraid of," Kalina muttered.

"I need to get home. I'm on shift tomorrow," Alex announced and Jimmy followed his brother out.

Kalina barely stifled a yawn as they left. It had been a busy day and she'd been running on adrenaline more than she'd realized. She rubbed at her eyes and yawned again. Time to go home and sleep on the information she'd gathered. Maybe things would make more sense in the morning. Before she turned out the lights and headed home she set a reminder in her phone to check city planning records in the morning.

12

The next morning Kalina woke with a headache. It had taken far too long to fall asleep the night before and her dreams were filled with disparate pieces of the Thomas Chase puzzle. She dragged herself out of bed and into the kitchen for a much needed cup of coffee. Her phone beeped at her to remind her of the task she'd set. Thankfully, the town made all building plans digital when they were approved; it made fact checking as easy as a couple mouse clicks.

She downed her first cup of caffeine in record time, pouring herself a second cup before she settled in front of her laptop in the living room. She had to move some boxes off the couch so she had a place to sit.

"OK, let's see what we've got," she muttered to herself and found the listing of most recently filed plans.

She didn't have to look very long before she found the plans for the condo and hotel layout. It loaded in a new tab and she had to blow it up to read any of it. She wasn't an expert with building plans but it was pretty obvious that the layout of the building stretched over a large section of the waterfront, including the Chase residence. In fact, it was right in the middle of the whole thing.

"Damn."

The little pieces of information she'd been gathering were all starting to fall into place now. The developer had likely hired Thomas because they needed his land to build the hotel and they thought getting him to collect on debts would get them what they wanted. Whether they expected his neighbors to turn on him and run him out of town or some other scenario, they likely counted on him handing things over to them before long. She doubted they'd intended to kill him. The guilty party could have been one of his neighbors but it didn't explain the gun registered in his name. Perhaps a trip to the only pawn shop in town was a good idea. She also wanted to head back out to the waterfront and see if she could talk to anyone whom Thomas might have tried to collect from.

Kalina forced herself to eat something before racing off for her day of investigation. Her curiosity was so overpowering at times that she forgot to eat. But fainting in the middle of things wasn't going to do anyone any good—least of all her—so she hastily downed a banana and some soggy oatmeal before heading out to her first stop. The pawn shop sat on the edge of town closest to the highway. In fact, it wasn't that far from her sister's place now that she thought about it. The parking lot was small—only three poorly marked spaces in front of the dimly lit front window. It gave her the creeps but she squared her shoulders and strode in.

"Well, I never thought I'd see you set foot in here," a deep baritone said from behind the front counter.

Blake Jansen had been a few years ahead of her in school and, much like her, had inherited the family business. He was big but in a non-threatening way. It was all belly fat and smile lines.

"Hey, Blake. How's it going?"

"It's going. I hear your place is hopping."

"People love their comics and nerdy stuff."

"What can I do for you today?"

"You may not be able to tell me but I was wondering if you know Thomas Chase."

"Real estate guy? Yeah, he helped my parents sell their place before they moved down south."

"His wife asked me to check if he'd been in to buy or sell anything recently. They came into some money recently and she's just worried he might be trying to sell off some antiques."

"Nope. Can't say that I've ever seen him in here."

"Really? Because she said she also found a gun case in his closet."

"Well, if he bought a gun, it wasn't through me. That I'd remember. There isn't anyone less likely to come into this place than him."

"Does anyone else work at the shop besides you? Maybe he came in when they were working?"

"I was out a few days last month with the flu. Had my cousin's kid cover for me. I'll check the receipts for you."

Kalina leaned on the countertop. "Thanks.

I know his wife will really appreciate it. I'm just hoping to put her mind at ease."

"How do you know the current Mrs. Chase?" Blake asked as he pulled a rolodex of cards from beneath the counter.

"She was friends with my sister in college."

"That so?" He flipped through some cards.

"Why? Is there something I should know about her?"

Blake shrugged and continued to sort through the cards. "I heard she majored in theater. Fancied herself something of an actress. If she's worried her husband's been pawning stuff, I wouldn't necessarily believe her."

"I didn't know that."

"Yep. I was honestly surprised she married Mr. Chase. I never thought he quite got over his first wife and I can't say I see what he does in her." He stopped flipping. "Well, I'll be damned."

Kalina tried to lean over to read the card he now held in his hand. The handwriting was too tiny and slanted for her to get a good look upside down.

"What is it?"

"Says he bought a handgun last month." Blake handed over the card for her to look at.

She pointed to the bottom of the card. "Is this his signature?"

"Looks like it. I guess I was wrong about them both. Sorry to say."

"Thanks. You've been really helpful. Do you mind if I take a picture of this just so I have proof for Savannah?"

"Normally I don't go handing things like this out unless there's a warrant involved but it can't hurt just this once."

Kalina whipped out her phone and snapped a picture, making sure to get a good image of the signature. She had been with Nadine when she'd signed the final documents with Thomas on the Larrabees' family home and this signature looked slightly off. After her next stop she'd definitely share what she'd learned with Chris. As much as she hated to admit how cliché it sounded, she was beginning to suspect that Savannah had a hand in Thomas's death.

"Thanks again for your help," she said before heading back to her car and the fresh air.

Armed with this new knowledge, she made the short trip to the waterfront and started browsing for houses with foreclosure and for sale signs until she spotted Leslie Mayfair sitting on her front porch with a for sale sign stuck into the small front lawn. Kalina would have preferred someone else to question but this was what had presented itself. It wasn't Kalina's fault that Leslie's former fiancé had turned out to be a vengeful murderer.

"Hi, Leslie," Kalina greeted as she left the driver side door open.

"Oh hi."

Kalina gestured toward the sign. "I didn't know you were moving."

"I was. The bank was going to foreclose but…"

"What happened?"

"The man they sent to collect on my debts offered to forgive them completely. He said he respected me and the value I add to this town too much to force me out."

"He just forgave them," she snapped, "just like that?"

"Yes."

"That wasn't Thomas Chase was it?"

Leslie nodded. "How'd you know?"

"I'd heard he'd gone into debt collection."

"Well, he said it sickened him what the town was doing with the development company. He said I wasn't the only person he had forgiven. Since the bank doesn't have any claim on this place anymore I don't have to move."

"And I'm guessing they can't build the hotel and condos if you're still here."

"Nope."

"I never said I'm sorry about what happened over the summer."

Leslie's eyes shone with unshed tears but she smiled. "I don't blame you, you know. I should have seen what was going on right in front of my face. The man I loved wasn't real. Just a façade."

"Still, it wasn't fair that he ruined your life too."

"I appreciate that." Leslie stood up and smoothed out the creases in her pants. "Can I ask why you were asking about Mr. Chase?"

"I realized I've been so busy getting my life sorted out I didn't know what was happening in town and I felt I should take more of an interest. This is home, after all."

Leslie glanced around the property and sighed. "Yeah, it is." With a grin she crossed the short distance to the sign and yanked it free, tossing it aside.

Kalina turned to get back into her car when she caught a hulking figure in the distance. She had an idea who would be lurking around this area and it sent shivers up and down her spine.

Kalina slid back behind the wheel and closed the driver side door. Time to tell Chris everything. Just as she reached for her phone, it began to buzz along the passenger seat with an incoming call: Jillian.

"Hey, look, I'm sorry I butted in earlier," she said after hitting 'Accept'.

"Forget that. Your boyfriend's little shadow, Jimmy, just showed up and arrested Savannah."

"What? Why?"

"I don't know. They won't tell me anything. This is insanity. She couldn't have killed her husband."

"Get her to call a lawyer. I'm going to the station to try to find out what's going on. I promise."

"A lawyer. God, this can't be happening."

"Jillian, stay calm. We're going to sort this out. You just need to stay level headed and don't get in their way."

"Fine. Just hurry and get there. Please," her sister pleaded.

Kalina revved the engine and did a quick U-turn at the end of the street, tires squealing as they tried to catch traction on the road. She raced up the street and caught sight of Mr. Mackland still lurking. Her heart thumped painfully against her ribs until he was out of sight in her rearview mirror.

Her thoughts raced as she made her way to

the station. What could they have arrested Savannah for? Had they found incriminating evidence in the $30,000 or some fingerprint on the gun? She pulled into the station parking lot and killed the engine. Before she could unbuckle her seatbelt, a second car came screaming into the lot and pulled in beside her, far too close for her to get out of her car without scratching the paint. She grabbed her phone and, as covertly as possible, hit Chris's number on speed dial. He might already be in with Savannah but maybe she'd get lucky and they were waiting for a lawyer to show up. She tried to ease the driver side door open but the driver of the other car stepped out and loomed large: Mr. Mackland. She glanced at her phone to see that it had connected and then placed it in her pocket. She eased her door shut and rolled down the window despite the chill that was settling over the day.

"Excuse me, I need to get out," she said as

politely as possible. She thought she heard Chris's muffled voice from her pocket.

"What were you doing talking to Ms. Mayfair?"

"That's none of your business."

"It is my business if it affects my employer's business plan."

"Well, that's not my fault. Leslie and I are friendly. You may not have heard but she had a bit of a rough time over the summer. Her fiancé was arrested for murder. I wanted to check on her and see how she was doing."

Mr. Mackland shrugged one beefy shoulder and slid his hand into his pocket, pushing the edge of his suit jacket back far enough to show her the gun holstered underneath his armpit. Her mouth went dry.

"You've been nosing around things that don't concern you." His tone implied the threat of the weapon he carried.

She pulled her phone out of her pocket as

if it had just started to ring with a call. "Hi, Detective Harper."

"Kal, what's going on? I'm about to go into an interrogation, here."

"I needed to stop by and see you but a Mr. Victor Mackland from Carlisle Premiere Developments won't let me get out of my car."

Mr. Mackland stayed where he was, not even flinching at the mention of Chris's title. Kalina tried to stare him down without showing fear but she doubted it was very effective.

"I'll be right out."

"Great. Thanks."

She hung up but kept the phone in view. She tried to keep her breathing even for the thirty seconds it took Chris to make his way out to the parking lot. Her pulse slowed a little at the sight of him. At least now she didn't have to worry about the thug pulling his gun on her. He couldn't be that reckless.

"Are you Mr. Mackland?" Chris asked and stopped mere inches from the man.

"I am."

"You need to move your vehicle and let Ms. Greystone get out of her car. I'd hate to have her file a harassment complaint against you."

"She's been snooping around where she doesn't belong."

"That still doesn't give you the right to intimidate her. Now move your car or I'll move it for you. Do I make myself clear?"

Mr. Mackland glanced between the two of them before he let out a grunt and stormed around to the driver side of his car and backed up enough for Kalina to get out. She rolled the window up and climbed out, throwing her arms around Chris without thinking.

"Thank you. He has a gun," she whispered in his ear.

"Go inside. I'll handle this."

She pulled away a little before saying, "I have to show you something about the case. It's important."

"When I'm done here you can show me."

"Please be careful." She gave him a quick kiss on the cheek before heading inside.

14

———

*J*illian sat at Chris's desk and Savannah was nowhere in sight. Kalina assumed she'd already been taken to the interrogation room. For once, the monitor showing the room was turned off. Kalina pulled a chair next to her sister and let out an anxious breath.

"They haven't questioned her yet. She asked for a lawyer," Jillian said, her tone flat.

"Good. I just had a run-in with a security guy from the developer."

"What do you mean?"

"I took a drive to the waterfront to see what's been going on and I talked to Leslie Mayfair. This security guy, Victor Mackland, followed me back here. I met him the day after Thanksgiving while Savannah was giving her statement about the break-in. He threatened me just now. Chris is handling it."

"Threatened you?" Jillian took Kalina's hand, going into protective older sister mode. "Did he touch you? Are you OK?"

"I'm fine. It was more an implied threat. He made sure I could see he had a gun. But I'd called Chris so he knew what was going on. I think I've figured some things out about Thomas's death. I just need Chris to get back in here so I can tell him. It might help Savannah."

"You know sometimes I don't know why he lets you poke around in his cases."

"Because I'm helpful? And I don't really mean to poke around, I just get curious and have to know what happened. He appreciates it, even if he doesn't say so."

On cue, Chris reappeared through the front door of the station. He held a business card by the tips of his fingers. "Jimmy! Get the fingerprint kit," he called before approaching his desk.

Kalina cleared a spot for him to work and noted Victor Mackland's name on the card. "What happened?"

"I told him politely if he ever went near you with a loaded firearm again I'd arrest him."

"Thanks. What's with the fingerprint kit?"

"I have a hunch."

"Can I tell you what I found out?"

Chris glanced at Jillian who promptly stood up and made herself scarce. Kalina took the spot her sister vacated and pulled up the photo of the paperwork from the pawn shop on her phone.

"So, after you mentioned that Mr. Chase

had a gun registered to him, I paid Blake Jansen a visit. He said someone came in and bought a gun under Mr. Chase's name." She enlarged the photo of the signature. "I'm no expert but I've seen Thomas Chase sign his name once or twice and this looks off."

"You think someone bought it using his name."

"Yes."

Chris brushed excess fingerprint powder into the trash and held up the card with a fresh print on it. "We found prints on the gun and the spray can that don't match Mr. or Mrs. Chase."

"And you think it was Mackland."

"I'm beginning to." He stuck the card in an evidence bag and scribbled information onto the label. "Jimmy, get this to the lab and tell them to rush it."

Jimmy grabbed the bag and disappeared. She could tell they both wished they had equipment to check the print themselves but the department was still strapped.

"There's more," Kalina said and set down her phone. "I think I might know why someone would want Mr. Chase dead and why Mr. Mackland would be involved."

Chris leaned back in his chair and steepled his fingers beneath his chin. "I'm listening."

"He was working for the developer as a debt collector. They needed to force people out of their houses so they could seize the property to build their new project. Basically, he offered to wipe people's debts clean if they paid part of their debt and he pocketed the difference between what they paid and what he bought the debt for."

"I understand how debt collection works, Kal."

She felt color warm her cheeks. "Well, it sounds like Thomas got fed up with the debt collecting life because he was forgiving loans for people who have property in strategic locations that really mess with building plans."

"That certainly establishes a motive and would also explain why Mr. Mackland was looming around the scene the other day."

"And why he came after me," she added.

"Right."

The conversation died when a middle-aged man in a faded blue suit appeared in their peripheral vision carrying a briefcase. He stopped momentarily at the front desk before approaching Chris's desk.

"I'm here for Savannah Chase," he said.

"She's in the interrogation room. I'll be with you in a moment."

Kalina craned her neck to follow the attorney's path into the room. "Why'd you arrest Savannah?"

"Mr. Mackland isn't the only one with a motive."

He disappeared without another word.

She waited until he closed the door to the interrogation room before she flipped the switch on the monitor. She tuned out the pleasantries and turned to the computer in front of her. She didn't know why she hadn't thought to check property records before but it would be easy enough to see who held the title to the Chase home. A quick search revealed what Chris likely already knew—Savannah owned the home and had been transferred the deed about six months after she married Thomas. The dead man's name drew Kalina's attention back to the interview.

"We found a receipt in your home for thirty thousand dollars. You said before that Thomas didn't have that kind of money."

Savannah glanced at her attorney and then said, "No. I mean we weren't poor by any means but that kind of lump sum would have been noticed in our joint account. Believe me; I keep an eye on it."

"I'm sure you do."

"You come from a fairly wealthy background yourself, don't you, Mrs. Chase?"

"I don't know what you mean."

"Your relatives were well off and you received a pretty hefty inheritance a few years ago."

"So?"

"We traced the money transfer that was sent to Carlisle Premiere Developments. The money originated in your account."

"Then maybe Thomas accessed it without me knowing."

"You are the only name on the account and we called the bank. You are the only person who could have authorized a transfer out of the account. Why did you want Thomas to take the debt collection job?"

"I didn't."

"Mrs. Chase, you need to stop lying now. You authorized the payment so Thomas could buy the debt collection package. He didn't seem the type to get into the business of shaking people down. So the pressure had to come from somewhere else. Like you."

Kalina pulled herself away from the questioning when she felt a presence behind her. She turned slowly to find Jimmy standing off to one side.

"Did you know their house was in the middle of the building zone?" Kalina asked.

"It's all making sense now. Huh."

"I'm assuming Chris knows that. And that she owns the house outright."

The color drained from Jimmy's cheeks and he started for the interrogation room.

"Uh, Jimmy, you might want to pick up that stuff on the printer first," Kalina said after hitting print on the land records and the building plans.

He gave her a nervous smile and headed into the room, appearing on the monitor moments later.

"Sir, I thought you should see these," Jimmy said and handed over the information.

Chris took the printouts and flipped through them. Kalina waited with baited breath for him to act. It wasn't that she wanted Savannah to be guilty but everything was pointing that way. Then again, maybe Blake was right and she'd gone into her marriage to Thomas with ulterior motives. Chris set the papers down in front of him and turned to Jimmy before standing up.

"Detective, what are you doing?" Jimmy's face failed to mask his confusion.

"This is your information, Jimmy. I think you should question our witness about what you found."

Kalina smiled as Chris stepped back and let Jimmy sit down. Jimmy would become a good cop one way or another and it made her a little proud to know she had a hand in it. Jimmy licked his lips and clasped his hands in front of him on the table.

"Well ... Mrs. Chase we've found records that show your home is in the middle of the development zone."

"What information is that?" her attorney asked.

Jimmy slid the printout of the zoning plan across the table and waited while the lawyer looked it over.

"And we also found out that you own the home outright. We have the land records that show Mr. Chase transferred the deed to you two years ago." He slid the second page across the table.

"Is there a question, Officer?"

"Well, it just seems suspicious that your husband would work for the people who are trying to buy out the rest of that area and then end up dead. I mean I suppose with him gone, there's no one to protest when you sell the house. I mean, if it were me, that's what I'd do."

"I didn't kill anyone," Savannah said quietly.

"But you know who did. And we think you had knowledge of it beforehand. If you tell us everything you know, we'll talk to the prosecutor about being lenient," Chris said from his spot by the door.

Even over a monitor, Kalina could see the color drain from Savannah's cheeks. Her shoulders hunched and she suddenly looked very frail. Her attorney looked between Jimmy and Chris and then loudly cleared his throat.

"I'd like a minute to speak with my client."

"Of course," Chris said.

He and Jimmy left the room and shut the door behind them. Kalina tried to look as if she hadn't been eavesdropping but Chris fixed her with a half-smile.

"Thank you for that information," he said.

"That was all Jimmy."

Jimmy opened his mouth to contradict her

but stopped and blushed. "Just trying to do my job."

"Either way, I think she's going to confess."

"You think she'll identify Mackland as being involved? I wouldn't put it past him to kill Thomas if he was really going against the company's orders," Kalina said.

"I'm pretty sure whatever she tells us will be enough to get a warrant for his arrest."

She nodded and silence settled between the three of them. Kalina caught glimpses of Savannah huddled in with her attorney. She glanced around the station, suddenly wondering what had become of her sister.

"I think your sister went outside," Jimmy offered, as if reading her thoughts.

"Thanks. I should go check on her. I think she's been taking this whole thing personally. She did always have a flair for the dramatic."

The door to the interrogation room opened behind them and Savannah's attorney appeared, motioning for them to come back in. Kalina bit her lip, torn between hearing Savannah's confession and checking on Jillian. If she was quick she might be able to do both. On a hunch, she headed out the front of the building. Jillian sat on a bench to the right of the entrance.

"Hey," Kalina said and sat down beside her.

"What's going on?"

"It looks like Savannah was involved in what happened to Thomas. I think she might be confessing."

"But she's not a killer."

"They think someone else killed him but she might have details about who that is. I'm sorry that you got dragged into all this."

Jillian let out a bitter laugh. "Don't apologize. She was my friend. She came to me and I let her into my home, offered her support."

"People change. And they do things for all kinds of reasons. Neither of us knows what was going on in her life or her marriage to prompt her agreeing to let someone murder her husband."

"I want to know why she did it."

Kalina offered a hand to her sister. "Come on. We can watch from the bull pen. I think you need some closure as much as Thomas."

15

The sisters walked back inside hand in hand. It appeared they hadn't missed much at all. Jimmy was just settling into another chair beside Chris. Savannah's cheeks were flushed and she kneaded her hands together nervously.

Chris leaned back in his chair. "So what has your client decided?"

"I'll tell you what I know." She sat up a little straighter and licked her lips. "A couple months back, the head of the development company came around our neighborhood and offered to buy a bunch of people out so they could build the condos. Thomas said no like most everyone else. I wasn't home when they came by the first time so I didn't know how much was being offered."

"I'm guessing it was a pretty nice sum."

"More than the house was worth. Thomas got it appraised every couple of years. He says it's out of habit. It was in his family for three generations. His grandfather built it maybe seventy years ago. He took full ownership around the time he married his first wife. When we married he put the deed in my name."

"Why did he do that?" Chris asked.

"He said that, since life is so short, he didn't want me to be without a place to live if something were to happen to him." Tears spilled down Savannah's cheeks. She let them fall, hands still clasped in front of her.

"What happened next?" Chris prompted.

Savannah took a shaky breath. "The developer sent a man to try to convince us to sell."

"This man?" Chris held his phone out.

Kalina couldn't see what he was showing her but she had to assume he'd managed to snap a picture of Victor Mackland.

"Yes, that's him." She dabbed at her eyes. "I don't know ... I guess they thought if we went along with it, other people might follow suit. But Thomas was still against selling. When the man came by again, he offered Thomas the opportunity to work for them and in exchange they'd pay him anything he wanted for the house. I told him he should take the job, work for a little while and then we'd cash out. They wanted thirty thousand dollars for the debt package. We didn't have that kind of money."

"Not jointly. You had it in your inheritance."

"I told Thomas we could use my money

but it meant he had to take the job and do what they said."

"Did you know he was going to die?" Jimmy interrupted.

Savannah shook her head. "No, I swear. Last week Thomas came home and told me that he was done working for them and he'd been forgiving loans. I don't know how but maybe Mr. Mackland was following him because they found out. Mr. Mackland contacted me and said we needed to keep Thomas in line. He said he'd handle it. He was just supposed to talk to Thomas. Scare him a little bit."

"And instead he ends up dead."

"I swear I really was going to report him missing when I came in. I lied about when I'd seen him last but I really was worried."

"What did you get out of this, besides being able to sell the property without him objecting?"

"They were going to pay me three times

what the house was worth. I could go any-where; do anything I wanted with that money. I'm not proud of it but it's the truth."

Chris drummed his fingers on the metal table for a beat and then leaned back again. "We didn't find any prints in the house when we searched after the break-in. Were you involved?"

Back in the bull pen Jillian shook her head, tears of her own shining in her eyes. Kalina kept a firm grip on her sister's hand the whole time but she could still feel Jillian's hand trembling in her own.

"I just don't understand. She had money."

"Sometimes people get greedy, Jill. And maybe she felt she had no other choice. I've met Mr. Mackland, remember."

Back in the interrogation room, Savannah let out a slow breath. "On Thanksgiving night I got a text from Mr. Mackland telling me to meet him at my house. He said we needed to make it look like someone broke in. I don't know why since I thought that would lead the police to look into what Thomas was doing but I didn't argue. I trashed the place myself. I thought I'd gotten rid of the bank transfer receipt but obviously not."

"So Mr. Mackland orchestrated everything."

"Yes. That's right."

"Would you be willing to sign an affidavit to that effect so we can arrest him?"

"She'll do whatever you need," her attorney said before Savannah could protest.

"Thank you, Counselor. Sit tight and we'll be back."

Chris stood up and Jimmy followed him out of the room, leaving the door ajar. Kalina let go of her sister's hand and closed the distance between her and Chris.

"So what happens now?"

"We draft the affidavit, she signs it and we get a warrant for this guy's arrest."

"That's it?"

"Right now, yeah, that's it."

"What will happen to Savannah?" Jillian asked.

"That's up to the prosecutor. She's a cooperating witness so that helps her. She may not face any jail time but I can't say for sure."

Kalina put a hand on Jillian's arm in the hopes of getting her sister out of Chris's way. He didn't have the time to waste talking to them. Not when a killer was still on the loose.

"Come on, Jill. Let's go home and let them do their jobs. There's nothing else we can do here."

Jillian nodded mutely and started for the front of the building. Before Kalina got two steps, Chris's hand wrapped around her wrist, arresting her momentum.

"Can you come by tonight? There's something I need to talk to you about."

"Sure."

"Good. I'll see you later." He kissed her on the lips.

The gesture made her cheeks warm—not just because it was a sudden moment of passion—and she had to pull away to catch her breath.

"Get this guy."

"I promise."

16

The parking lot seemed oddly empty as they walked out into the afternoon air. Kalina started for her car—intent on following her sister home to make sure she didn't have a nervous breakdown at the revelation that her close friend was capable of selling out her spouse for money—but stopped when she noted her back tires were slashed.

"You've got to be kidding me," she groaned.

"Do you think that Mr. Mackland did this?" Jillian said from behind her.

"Who else would try to keep me from leaving?" She pulled out her phone and hit Chris's name on speed dial.

It rang once before he answered. "Forget something?"

"No, someone slashed my tires."

"And by someone you mean our murder suspect?"

"Yes."

"Come back in and we'll file a report.

"No, I'll catch a ride home with Jillian. You need to focus on catching this guy for the bigger crime. My car will survive."

"I'd feel better if you filed a report."

"I promise I'll do that as soon as you have the guy in custody."

"Fine."

"Oh, it's just a hunch but you should try looking for this creep at the developer's main office. It's the address on the business card he gave me the other day."

"Will do."

She ended the call. Jillian shifted from foot to foot, waiting for something else to happen. Kalina flashed her sister a smile. "Come on, you should go home. Spend some time with Dan and AJ. After all, I gave him the weekend off so you could hang out as a family."

"You talked to Dan didn't you?" her sister said as they walked side by side to her car.

"Maybe."

Together they checked to ensure that her car was intact before climbing in and making the short journey to Jillian's place. Jillian put the car in park and cut the engine but didn't move from her spot behind the wheel.

"You're going to be okay," Kalina said and patted her sister's hand.

"I know. It's really selfish of me to even feel

betrayed or hurt. I'm worried about what's going to happen to Savannah.'

"You heard Chris. The prosecutor will likely give her a deal. She might not even see any jail time."

"She's ruined here though. She can't stay. Everyone is going to know what happened."

"I sort of got the feeling she didn't want to stay here anyway."

"I suppose you're right."

"Jill, I'm sorry this happened. It's never easy finding out the people we thought we knew and could trust aren't the people we thought they were."

"I guess we're all learning that the hard way."

"Yeah. Come on, let's go inside. I think we could both use a drink."

"It's the middle of the day."

"It's a weekend and it's been one hell of a couple days. We deserve it."

They both climbed out and headed up the

front steps. Jillian dug her key out of her purse. "I'll get the glasses."

Kalina kicked off her shoes upon entering the house and headed straight for the living room. Daniel and AJ were nowhere to be seen. Just as Jillian returned with a bottle of white and two glasses, footsteps thundered down the stairs and AJ appeared.

"Hey, what's going on? I thought we were supposed to be doing this whole family time thing this weekend."

"Your aunt solved the case," Jillian said, growing misty eyed.

"Not really. Well, maybe I helped a little."

"Stop being modest, Aunt K. You probably cracked the case wide open." He settled on the couch between them—taking up far more space than a teenage boy should be able to—and fiddled with the cork from the wine bottle. "So what happened?"

"I don't really think—" Jillian began.

"He's going to find out when it hits the news," Kalina interrupted.

"I guess you're right. Savannah was involved. She didn't kill her husband but she knew a very dangerous man was trying to threaten him."

"Why?"

"For money. She was promised a lot of it if she cooperated with getting people to leave so the development could be built."

Kalina let out a bitter laugh. "I have a feeling the project won't be going forward any time soon."

"Good. Then people won't have to move."

"Exactly." Kalina took a long sip of wine and let it burn down her throat. She'd needed it more than Jillian to calm her nerves. She hadn't wanted to admit it but she was scared of Victor Mackland. She had no doubt he'd be out of their lives soon but until he was in handcuffs and carted away she couldn't relax.

She was so lost in her thoughts she didn't

hear her phone ring. AJ nudged her in the thigh, causing her phone to dig into her leg. She yanked it out and saw a missed call from Chris's cell phone.

"Excuse me."

She extricated herself from the couch, set her wineglass down on the table and retreated to the kitchen for some privacy. She hit redial and waited while the line connected.

"Hi, sorry I missed you," she said when he picked up.

"I wanted to let you know we have Mackland and his boss in custody. It looks like he's going to be fairly cooperative with us. His boss was already starting to talk on the ride back to the precinct."

"That's great. You have no idea how much better I feel right now."

"We still need you to file a report about your tires."

"You know what; it's not even worth it. I'll

get new tires. It's not a big deal. Focus on making the murder charges stick to this guy."

"If things go well I should be able to get away in a couple hours."

"Why don't I come by the house around seven?" Kalina offered.

"That sounds perfect. I'll see you then. I love you, Kal."

"I love you too."

Kalina couldn't keep a smile from spreading across her lips. The danger was past. If he was willing to confess easily, it made Chris's job much easier. She returned to the living room and Jillian's face brightened instantly.

"Good news I take it?"

"They have him in custody and it sounds like he's going to confess. This whole mess is going to be over."

"Oh, thank God!" Jillian tipped the bottle over her glass until it was almost overflowing.

Kalina grabbed the bottle before it spilled

and drained the rest of it into her own glass. The raised them in a toast and she took a long drink. This time it didn't burn on the way down. A few minutes later they both set down empty glasses and Jillian pulled Kalina into a hug.

"I'm so glad you were on this one, Kal. I couldn't have handled all of this without you. I'm sorry I was so bitchy before. I love you."

"You're forgiven, Jill. And I love you too."

Normally, this much show of affection from her older sister would have made Kalina uncomfortable but the relief that washed over Jillian's face made it bearable. Now she could look forward to whatever Chris needed to tell her tonight.

17

Seven o'clock came far faster than Kalina expected. She'd gotten AJ to give her a ride home so she could change with enough time to walk to what would soon be her house. On the way over, her phone buzzed with a call from her mother. Guilt twisted Kalina's gut at the realization that neither she nor Jillian had been keeping their mother apprised of what was happening.

"Hi, Mom," she said and slowed her pace to a stroll.

"Hi sweetheart. How are you?"

"I'm OK. I'm sorry I didn't check in after Thanksgiving. Friday was really busy at the shop."

"It always was for your father too."

"I'm sorry we didn't keep you in the loop on what happened with Thomas Chase."

"Your sister filled me in just now. How horrible. A part of me feels bad for that young woman but the rest me is just disgusted that she'd agree to coerce a man she claims to love into doing something against his principles."

"Yeah. You think you know someone and then this happens. I think Jill is taking it harder than she's letting on. But we can be there for her."

"Yes, of course. Honey, you sound a little winded. Are you sure you are all right?"

"Yes, Mom, I'm fine. I'm just walking to Chris's."

She could almost hear the smile in her

mother's voice. "You're going to have to stop calling it his house soon."

"I know." The squat, two-story house came into view and it sent excited shivers down her spine. "I'm here. I should go."

"I love you."

"Love you too."

Kalina ended the call and stowed her phone in her purse. Checking her hair in the glass inlaid in the front door, she rang the bell and waited. She spotted Chris through the glass and beamed at him when he opened the door.

"Right on time," he said and pulled her in for a kiss.

He was certainly being more affectionate than normal. He must have really felt guilty for missing Thanksgiving. He finally pulled away, leaving her breathless.

"Can I get you something to drink? A glass of wine or coffee?"

"I think that depends on what you need to

talk to me about. Should I be sober for this conversation?"

Chris's brow furrowed for a moment as the overhead light caught the strands of gold laced through his hair. "Coffee's better."

"Then, sure, I'll have some coffee."

He smiled at her and disappeared into the kitchen. She made herself comfortable on the couch and studied the room. They'd brought over some smaller items like pictures already. Even these little touches made the place feel like home already.

"Here you go," he said, handing her a mug.

She gripped it between both hands and inhaled the aroma. "So did everything go well at the station?"

"He confessed to everything including slashing your tires."

"Guilty conscience?"

"He doesn't strike me as the guilty feeling type. I think he realized there was nowhere to go and no one to protect him. The head of the company also confessed to his part in everything. The project is going to be shut down."

"Good. I'm glad everything worked out."

"Yeah." He took a slow sip from his mug and set it on the table. He turned to face her and pulled one of her hands from her mug to cradle between both of his. "I really am sorry I missed Thanksgiving."

"It's fine. You had work, I understand that. Besides, there will be other Thanksgivings and Christmases to spend with my family."

He gave her hand a squeeze but stayed silent.

"Chris, what is it?"

He relinquished his grip with his right hand; it dipped into his pants pocket, producing a small box. "I'd planned to do this on Thanksgiving. Your mom and sister were in on the whole thing too." He opened the box. "Kalina Greystone, will you marry me?"

Sound fell away and all she could see was

the delicate diamond ring nestled in the jewelry box. Of all the things he could have said, she wasn't expecting a proposal. They'd been together less than six months. But even though their time together again was short, her heart told her she was ready. Their history had led them to this very moment.

"Kalina? Did you hear me?"

She blinked and the world came rushing back. Clumsily, she set down the coffee mug and threw her arms around him, kissing whatever part of him she could reach. "Yes. Of course the answer's yes!"

"It is?"

She leaned back to give him a proper kiss on the lips. The kiss bubbled over into a fit of laughing when she caught the surprise on his face. "Of course. We're moving in together. Why would I say no?"

"I don't know ... maybe you thought it was too fast?"

"We've been working towards this since

high school, Chris. I think we're ready. Besides, I think we both know there's no one else out there for us."

His shoulders relaxed and he slid the ring —a perfect fit—onto her finger. The diamond caught the light from the table lamps and sparkled merrily from its new perch. She curled up in his arms and sighed with contentment. This was the perfect way to end a crazy, hectic few days. Sure, a chapter of a man's life had come to an end but this one in hers was just being written.

"I can't believe my mom and Jillian kept this a secret." She laughed. "No, scratch that. I'm surprised AJ didn't find out and spill the beans ahead of time."

"I only wish I could have asked for your father's blessing."

A twinge of sadness pulled at her heart but it passed after a moment. Her father would have been proud of her for everything she'd accomplished in the last few months.

When brides are wishing up dead on the beach, can Kalina untangle the marital web before she ends up he next victim?
Download Have and Hold and chase he killer today.

GET FREE CONTENT

Sign up for my newsletter by clicking here to be kept up-to-date with my latest releases and receive your copy of Toil and Trouble as a free gift.

All Hallow's Eve brings dangerous secrets. Can Kalina get to the bottom of the mystery?

Subscribe and find out now!

A GEEKS AND THINGS COZY MYSTERY
Toil and Trouble
S.E. BIGLOW

ABOUT THE AUTHOR

S.E. Biglow is the pen name of *USA Today* bestselling author Sarah Biglow. She lives in Massachusetts with her husband and son. She is a licensed attorney and spends her days combatting employment discrimination as an

Investigator with the Massachusetts Commission Against Discrimination.

You can find an up-to-date list of all my books here